The Crystal Cavern

Sandra Miller

The Crystal Cavern

Published by Onda Mountain Books

Cover Art © Kriscole | Dreamstime.com

Copyright © 2010 by Sandra Miller.

This is a work of fiction. Names, characters, places and incidents either are the product of the author's imagination or are used fictitiously, and any resemblance to any actual persons, living or dead, events, or locales is entirely coincidental.

The Crystal Cavern

Short, choppy waves broke at Taran's feet as he squinted into the horizon. He shaded his strained eyes with his hand.

Manar smiled and shook his head. "Taran, my son, you won't be able to see it that way. I sent the buoy out on the tides yesterday morning."

Taran's ears burned. He should have known that. Squaring his shoulders, he closed his eyes and sent his mind out on the sea. Calm waters met him; the red training buoy was immediately obvious. He opened his eyes with a long whistle. "It's gone quite far out."

"Yes. Can you pull it in?"

Taran frowned. "Father, wouldn't it be simpler just to....to *bring* it here, all at once?"

Manar's frown matched that of his nearly-adult son. "What you speak of is sorcery, Taran. No wizard has ever cast a successful sorcery. I, for one, am not convinced any wizard should try. It is not a natural thing."

Taran considered that. "What is the difference between sorcery and wizardry?"

"That's an excellent question, Taran. While you bring in the training buoy, I'll go back to the house and take out the old books. When you come back with the buoy I'll explain it to you."

Taran nodded. Did Manar need time to study or to compose himself? He lifted a hand in farewell to his father. Manar started back toward the house, then suddenly turned and faced Taran. "For now, let's just say that the difference between them is that wizardry can be done. Sorcery can not." Manar turned again and left.

Taran sat down in the sand, his white apprentice robes spreading around him. The bright blue trim sparkled in the sunlight, and he studied it. His questions disturbed his father. *Wizardry can be done. Sorcery cannot.* With a sigh, Taran closed his eyes and concentrated. His eyelids fluttered as he sent out his mind, not in the manner he had been taught, but in the manner that was easiest for him. An immeasurably short time later, the buoy sat on the sand before him.

He sighed again, brushing his fingers across the smooth red surface. "Wizardry can be done. Sorcery cannot." He shrugged, then scooped up the buoy and started the long walk back to the house.

*****

"So you can see," said Manar, pacing as he talked, "how wizardry is fundamentally different from sorcery. Wizardry is-- well, what wizards do, and it involves the manipulation of natural forces." Manar paced stiffly, his tall lanky body moving somewhat awkwardly, as though he was not quite comfortable in it. Abruptly he sat down behind his big oak desk. "Now any wizard can be Light or Dark. A pyromancer can just as easily use his skills for destruction as for peace. But any wizard is limited to manipulation of the forces he specializes in. A geomancer could work with the forces of growth that occur in the earth to greatly speed the growth of a tree. But a geomancer could not just simply wave his hands and make a tree appear where there was no tree or sapling or seed before. Anything involving creating objects from nothing, making things just disappear, or casting illusions to make something appear as it is not is sorcery." Manar glanced at the clock on the wall. "Now you had better go wash up for dinner." He turned away and began cleaning the salt and sand from the buoy.

Taran turned to leave, wondering if he should try to explain to his father what he could do. He glanced over his shoulder at his father, still at work cleaning the buoy. Ocean grime still covered almost half of the training aid. Making things disappear, he reminded himself, is sorcery. Completely impossible. With a carefully restrained sigh he addressed Manar. "Father?"

Manar paused and looked up at his son. "Yes, Taran?"

Taran glanced at the buoy. "I wanted to thank you for answering my question."

Manar smiled. "Of course you are very welcome, my son. That is, after all, what I am here for."

Taran smiled in return. He turned away from the gleaming buoy and left, closing the study door quietly behind him.

*****

Sleep came quickly to Taran that night, but it was a tormented sleep. He tossed and turned restlessly, finally subsiding into weary stillness.

A cold, thick mist surrounds Taran. He can just barely see in the dim light.

"What in the name of the Light?" Taran turns in a slow circle, straining his eyes, but can see nothing through the mist. He reaches blindly and gropes around him, then takes a few stumbling steps forward, but finds nothing in the mist.

For a moment he simply stands there, feeling trapped and helpless. When the obvious finally hits him he hesitates a moment longer, chastising himself for his stupidity, before he closes his eyes and concentrates. His senses reach out around him. He has never seen a place so completely barren of anything at all.....but there is something....something he can't quite identify, something that brushes his inquiring senses aside before he can get a handle on it....far off to his left.

Taran opens his eyes and frowns. Never has he encountered something he couldn't sense....but this place seems to be full of things he has never encountered. Something is urging him to go and seek out this thing, to see with his eyes what he cannot see otherwise. He feels a vague sense of dread about doing that. Standing here letting his nerves get the best of him will not improve his situation, though, so with a deep breath he starts off.

In an amount of time far too short to cover the immense distance his senses indicated, he sees a steadily brightening light ahead. The mist seems to thin out, but that may be an effect of the light.

In a few more steps the light is bright enough to hurt his eyes, and he throws his arm up across them, peering out from under it as he takes a couple more staggering steps forward. Suddenly he halts, almost falling, squinting in the light that is painful even with his arm shading his eyes. In front of him towers an impossibly tall man dressed entirely in the black robes of a necromancer. Where has this man come from?

A second ago Taran was completely alone.

Squinting against the glare, he tries to study the figure in front of him. The necromancer is carrying a completely black staff, and the unbearably bright light is coming from behind him, silhouetting him in the swirling mist. Taran tries to discern some details of the man's appearance, but has to look down when his eyes water too intensely to focus.

The man laughs, a sound that resonates much more than it should. Taran's hair stands on end. "Blinded by the great Aseligan! So this is the little sorcerer, eh?" He falls silent a moment, surveying the uncomfortable youth, and Taran feels himself being examined with senses beyond the eyes. "Well, well," the figure continues in a musing tone, "you are a little firecracker, aren't you? Look, boy, does this light bother you?"

Struggling to function past his confusion, Taran manages somehow to nod.

"Yes, yes....I daresay it would. Don't just stand there, sorcerer-boy, do something about it!"

He realizes that he is being challenged. With a small theatrical wave that is solely for this strange individual's benefit, Taran cuts the lights to fully half of what they were.

The man in black smiles, a crooked, dangerous smile that does not inspire confidence. "Very good, young man, very good indeed...." The image of the necromancer is somehow fading. "You could cause me no end of problems. It is well that I found you early." The image is barely visible now. "I bid you farewell now, Taran--forever!"

Just in time, Taran catches sight of the towering wave rolling toward him, black and impenetrable. He throws himself to the ground, huddles in a ball, and instinctively casts a protective ward around himself. The wave crashes over him, battering him and rolling him, but the ward holds. He is surrounded by thick, oily matter. A smell *like death is thick in his nostrils, settling acridly sweet on his tongue, choking him.*

Taran jerked suddenly awake, looking sharply around, fully expecting to see a tall necromancer with a staff standing somewhere around. He let out a long breath and fell back against the pillows, shaking. The sheets were soaked with cold sweat, and his heart galloped.

It was only a dream, he told himself, trying to quell his panic. *Only a--*

A smell like death settled acridly sweet on his tongue, choking him.

He fumbled out of bed, clumsy with sudden fear. The stench was heavy in the back of his throat, and his stomach churned. If the terrible smell had been real, how much else of the dream had really happened? Who was Aseligan?

Where were his parents?

Gripped by irrational terror, he ran down the hall to his parent's room. "Mother! Father! I--"

He stopped short in the doorway, staring with disbelieving eyes at the half-rotten forms bulging beneath the quilts on the bed. The stench gagged him. He couldn't feel his hands.

Karran and Manar looked like things that had died several months ago. Rotten flesh hung in sickly flaps, and he could see the gleam of white bone in places. The quilts oozed with thick matter he dared not look at too closely.

Taran fell to his knees and vomited.

He made it back to his own room before the tears came. He no longer had to wonder what was in that oily wave Aseligan had launched at him. Pestilence. Concentrated pestilence had killed and decomposed his parents in a matter of moments.

He couldn't stay here. He pulled out his well-worn leather

satchel, and through his tears began to pack into it his few possessions. He took his blue staff out of his closet and regarded it a moment. The color of the staff indicated that his specialty was aquamancy, and he knew that was not appropriate. Things would be easier for him if he claimed a commonly accepted profession, but something compelled him to honesty, in this as in everything else. He considered a moment before changing the staff to black steel with brass fittings over the ends. The black worried him a little, for he didn't want to be mistaken for a necromancer. But necromancers didn't use brass on their staffs; no wizard did. And Taran couldn't think of a better way to indicate sorcery. He sat on the edge of the bed with his staff across his lap until his tears finally subsided.

When the sun began to rise he ventured out into Feldwar. He dreaded the explaining he would have to do, but he could not simply sneak away and be thought a murderer. He would take proper leave of the village, and see to it that his parents were buried with honor.

But he knew as soon as he stepped into the street that there would be no leave-taking. The cloying stench of death hung heavy over the homes and shops. Not a soul stirred in the village. Taran searched frantically through half a dozen little buildings before he finally accepted that Feldwar was no more. He leaned heavily on his staff, panting raggedly in the bright morning sunshine that seemed so out of place in this village of the dead.

"Light keep them," he murmured finally, and turned away. He was the sole survivor, a thought that brought with it guilt heavy enough to crush him. If he had but cast his ward wider, he could have saved his parents. Perhaps he could have saved them all. Tears burned the backs of his eyes as he plodded to the stables outside the village gates. His brother Renas lived in the town of

Caleb, and he had to be told. And if it took Taran until the last of his days, he would find that necromancer and avenge his people.

Nothing remained for him here. Quite possibly there was nothing for him anywhere. All he could do was go out on his own, and find out what he could do for himself. In a world where sorcery did not exist, he was a sorcerer and so where his skills were concerned he would always be alone.

*****

The cold wind lashed Taran's hair, and jerked his oilcloth loose. Rain spattered in on his arms. Sighing, he adjusted the waterproof cloth for the umpteenth time and patted his horse's neck. With the whipping wind behind it, the water seemed to find its way into every crevice. Using the skills his aeromancer mother taught him, Taran examined the clouds above, and shook his head. The rain would continue all day, and the next as well. There was no sign of it getting much heavier right away, though. He supposed that much was good, anyway. Nonetheless, that rain.... Caleb was a full two days' ride in good weather. With the rain, and the mess it would make of the dirt road, he would be lucky to make it in three. He wiped the moisture from his face and pulled his wide-brimmed hat down lower.

His thoughts turned again to Aseligan. Not much was known about him. He claimed necromancy as his specialty, and he was the single most powerful wizard of the Dark. He was probably the most powerful wizard of either type, but that was not usually said. And yet he thought Taran presented enough of a threat to wipe out his entire village in an attempt to be rid of him.

Tears dripped unheeded down Taran's face. What had he done to provoke such a ruthless attack? Why hadn't he realized the danger to the village and cast a wider ward? Darkness take it, he would have vengeance. For his parents, for his friends, for his village.

He intended to destroy the most powerful wizard alive. And he didn't even know the extent of his own capabilities.

Abruptly he pulled his thoughts out of their self-defeating cycle, and the sensation was like suddenly waking from a nap. The rain had lightened, but the wind was just as tempestuous and his gelding barely plodded along. Taran sighed. He struggled with the oilcloth and nudged Bryn back to a steady pace somewhere between a walk and a trot. The rain had almost stopped, and Taran took advantage of the break to dig a loaf of bread from a saddlebag. He gnawed his way through it, trying not to think about the hopelessness of his position.

*****

Dusk was falling when Taran set up camp in a clearing beside the road. He tethered Bryn to a nearby tree, and worked with some low hanging branches and a length of twine to turn his oilcloth into a crude shelter. He had to admit it wasn't much to look at, but it kept the rain out.

In front of him was a small, orderly pile of the driest wood he could find. He fumbled in his saddlebags for his flint box, until it occurred to him that he might not need them. Taran had never tried any pyromancy before. He concentrated on feeling the fibers of the wood, on bringing the forces of combustion to bear on the those. After several minutes of concentration, he opened his eyes. Nothing. Not even a spark. He sighed heavily. Pyromancy apparently wasn't one of his talents. Taran blew out his cheeks. With an air of resignation, he tried to light the fire drawing on the same power he had used to move the training buoy what felt like forever ago. It was more of an effort than he remembered, and he had to concede failure after a few minutes. He leaned back

13

with an exhausted gasp and tried to think, breathing heavily. Why couldn't he seem to--

His staff suddenly caught his eye, lying on the ground next to him. An eerie light surrounded it, as if the black steel was actually....glowing. Taran frowned. Moving as if his body was out of his control, he picked up the staff gingerly, and carefully touched one end to the stacked wood. Instantly flames burst forth, and although it was hard to be sure in the sudden light, it seemed to Taran the staff had stopped glowing.

Still frowning, he slowly sat down. This was really too much. He pulled another loaf of bread and a chunk of cheese from a saddlebag to serve as dinner and ate without really thinking about it. His sudden inability to cast spells was extremely disturbing.

At first he thought someone was interfering with him; perhaps Aseligan limiting his powers. But the strange behavior of his staff made him dismiss that idea. It was obvious that he needed something to focus his power through; in this case his staff. But what if he was separated from his staff? And why hadn't he had this problem at home? His staff had never left his closet at the house, and it obviously needed to be close at hand to serve as a focus. So how--

"Hallo the fire!" rang a clear voice. Distracted from his deep thought, Taran finally noticed the approaching horse's hooves that should have registered several minutes ago.

"Hallo and welcome," called Taran in return. He finished the last of his dinner and spread out his sleeping blankets. A chestnut mare approached, led by a redheaded young woman dressed in the brown leathers of a healer. "Good evening! Although I have to admit, with this rain there isn't much that's good about it," she added darkly, pushing her damp hair out of her face. "Mind if I join you?"

Taran had to smile. "Not at all. Let's get your horse taken care of and you can come in out of the rain," he said, catching up the bucket he used to water Bryn. They tended to the mare, then walked back to the camp in silence.

As soon as they were seated by the fire, she rummaged through her bags, finally producing a waxed paper packet of dried fruits.

"I'm Taran," he said by way of introduction. "Aquamancer and amateur aeromancer."

"Must be a Light-blessed pyromancer to get a fire started tonight," she commented, picking out a dried apple wedge and popping it in her mouth.

Taran smiled weakly, a little discomfited by this observation. "Well--you never know what you might be suited to do if you don't try."

She nodded. "Jendaline," she said without prelude. "I'm a healer."

"Not a good healer, or a great healer--just a healer?"

He was teasing her, trying to relieve some of the seriousness he suddenly sensed from her, and she grinned. "I suppose that averages out. The ones I can help think I'm a great healer--the ones I can't think I'm a witch. To the ones who aren't ill," she inclined her head toward Taran, "I'm just a healer."

"So, Jendaline Just-a-Healer, where are you headed?" Taran pulled two battered metal mugs from his bags and filled them with apple cider.

"Well--that's something of a tricky question, actually. Oh-- thank you," she said, accepting one of the mugs. "I'm headed to the first place I find that looks suitable to stay. Caleb is the first town on the road, so I guess that's my first stop."

The fire crackled as some of the burnt wood gave way, and the shifting of the stack sent sparks into the dirt at Taran's feet. He pulled at some of the wood at the edge, rearranging the pile into a more stable shape, then leaned back and took up his cider again. "Moving?"

Jendaline laughed, a harsh laugh with no humor. "Not by choice. My family made me rather....unwelcome, so I left." She shrugged philosophically. "I suppose I had it coming. Entirely my own fault, really."

Taran waited a moment for her to continue, wondering what sort of crime had caused her own family to turn on her. Had he been wise to invite her into his camp? He raised his eyebrows expectantly. "Why was that?"

She made a great show of looking around for eavesdroppers before answering. "I refused to conform to their beliefs. Shocking, isn't it? I made the obviously insane suggestion that healing and wizardry could be combined."

Taran considered that for a moment. Although healing wasn't usually referred to as a type of wizardry, it really was. "Well, why couldn't they? It sounds like a wonderful idea to me."

"It does to me, too, which is why I'm here instead of with my parents in Hommel. But it doesn't fit into their world view. According to them, each type of wizardry is separate and distinct from all the others, and completely opposed to one of them, in a sort of weird balance. Pyromancy versus aquamancy, geomancy versus aeromancy, necromancy versus healing. You combine them at your own peril, especially if they are opposing fields. I don't really understand the argument, I think, but they insist that a healer should be completely devoted to healing and completely free of wizardry. I think they are forgetting that healing is basically a form of wizardry anyway." She shook her head. "What a complex answer to a simple question, eh? 'Where are you headed?' 'I'm glad you asked. Let me tell you my life story....'"

She smiled self-deprecatingly. "So where are you headed?"

Taran wished he could warm his cider, but after his failure with the fire, he knew the effort would be wasted. "I'm headed for Caleb myself. I have a brother there, an aeromancer."

She nodded. "So you're moving, too?"

"Well, yes--I suppose I am. I don't know quite where to go, but I can't go back." He fell silent, staring into the fire and thinking about all the reasons he was there.

"I can certainly understand that." Jendaline stifled a yawn, and he sat up suddenly.

"I'm sorry," he said. "You must have had a long ride, and here I am keeping you up half the night. It's high time we went to sleep."

She nodded sleepily and unrolled her blankets. When she finished, Taran extinguished the fire and crawled under his own worn but clean quilts. Sleep did not come immediately and he stared up at the faint moonlight visible through the clouds, surprised at how open the sky seemed away from the village lights of Feldwar.

I can certainly understand that.... Jendaline's words echoed in his mind. He thought about his circumstances, and wondered just how much she would understand, when the time came that he must tell her.

*****

The two were on the road again shortly after sunrise the next morning. They had an unspoken agreement to ride on to Caleb together, an arrangement which was not only convenient but practical. And Taran had to admit he did enjoy her company, and riding in the rain with someone to talk to certainly beat riding in the rain brooding alone.

The rain subsided to a mist so fine that Taran bundled up his oilcloth in one of his saddlebags. The mist was irritating, but Taran preferred it and the breeze to the stuffiness and constant readjustment of the oilcloth. From time to time he had to brush the accumulated water from his clothes and boots, and Jendaline watched him with a smug smile. Her leather healer's robes were inherently waterproof. When she had to push her wet hair from her face, Taran tried to look equally smug as he flicked the water from his hat brim.

"I've been thinking," Taran said, pretending not to notice the glare Jendaline gave him for his attempt at smugness. "When you first mentioned it the idea sounded good, but the more I consider the ramifications of adding wizardry to healing, the more it sounds like a brilliant idea. You could use aquamancy to lower fevers quicker and easier than with herbs alone. Pyromancy could help fight infections, sterilize cuts...." Taran talked faster and faster, getting more and more excited about the idea. "With some geomancy you could grow the herbs you need for healing with much greater speed....even make them more potent...." He restrained himself from speculating further on the nearly endless possibilities of healing combined with wizardry. "It's really a stroke of genius--I mean, Jendaline, you could revolutionize the whole field of healing!"

Jendaline smiled. "I know, Taran. That is why I'm here; I couldn't find anyone back home who would teach me the basics of any field."

Taran tried to keep his mouth from falling open, and almost succeeded. "Not *anyone*? Even when you explained....?"

"Not anyone," she confirmed.

"But....couldn't they see?"

"I would assume so. But you have to understand, my parents are very influential in Hommel. And they sit on the town council....nobody wants to cross them." She sighed. "So I'm going to Caleb. Maybe people there will be more open-minded."

"I can't imagine they wouldn't be," Taran said. "Like I said last night, my brother Renas lives in Caleb. He is an aeromancer and I'm sure he would be glad to help."

She smiled as he wiped at the water on his clothes again, and averted her eyes when he gave her a mock-menacing frown.

*****

Rain slashed down as Taran and Jendaline rode into Caleb. Lightning flashed across the sky and thunder rumbled disconsolately every few seconds. Taran wore his oilcloth wrapped around him like a shroud, and Jendaline wore his hat. The sound of the rain pounding down made conversation impossible. They tethered their horses in front of a cottage with a white cloud decoration on the door, signifying an aeromancer's residence.

Renas showed no surprise when he answered their knock on the door. He looked from his brother to Jendaline and back, then invited them in with a knowing smile that Taran wasn't sure he appreciated.

"Renas," he said, dropping the wet oilcloth and hat in the reed basket by the door, "you're an aeromancer. Can't you do something about this damned rain?"

Renas laughed. He was taller than Taran, with a kind, gentle face that had seen many smiles. "You're an aquamancer, little brother--do something about it yourself." Jendaline lifted a hand to her face to conceal an involuntarily smile, and Renas laughed again. "Come on in and have a seat, you two."

They walked into Renas's small but well-furnished living room, and he turned to Jendaline just before she sat down. "I'm Renas," he said, casting a sidelong glance at Taran, "since my brother is going to insist on being rude and not introducing us."

He heaved a theatrical sigh. "Younger brothers are such a trial that way, but what can you do?" He shrugged and shook his head mournfully.

Taran flushed. "I'm sorry!" he blurted, just as Jendaline said, "I'm Jendaline; I'm a healer from Hommel, pleased to meet you."

"And now he is interrupting ladies," Renas said sternly, giving his brother a mock-disapproving look. "Clearly I shall have to beat him. A pity. Now Jendaline, would you like spiced cider, herb tea, or berry juice?"

"Berry juice, please," she said, taking a chair across the small table from Taran.

"Berry juice it is, then." Renas headed for the kitchen.

"Cider for me, please," Taran called at his older brother's departing back.

"I know, heathen. Always cider for you." His voice trailed off as he moved around in the kitchen.

Jendaline leaned back in the stuffed chair and sighed. "It feels so good to be off of a horse and in a comfortable chair again."

"I know," Taran agreed. "That was undoubtedly the longest three-day ride of my life." He considered a moment. "But the company was excellent."

Jendaline let that pass with a smile. "Your brother seems like a nice man, Tar."

Taran wondered why she chose to bring Renas up in that particular moment. He remembered the ability of an aeromancer to eavesdrop using air currents. "Yes. I usually just tell people he's an old galderbeast, but he's really not such a bad sort."

"You still think he will help me?"

"I'm positive." Taran hoped he was right.

Renas walked in with a brass serving platter in his hands and an expression far too placid to be genuine on his face. So he had been eavesdropping, then. He set the tray on the table and handed the ceramic mugs around without so much as a glance at his brother. "Now then," he said, sitting in the chair at the end of the table, "tell me what brings you to Caleb."

Taran and Jendaline exchanged a glance. Hoping to save his own story for a moment when he could be alone with his brother, he said , "Well--Jendaline could use your help...." He looked to Jendaline.

"Actually," she said, not quite meeting Renas's gaze, "I was wondering if you could teach me aeromancy--only the basics, I mean--you don't have to make any major commitment...."

"Jendaline is hoping to combine some wizardry with her healing," Taran explained. "It could really make healing much more powerful."

Renas sipped his tea, either considering or pretending to. Finally he nodded. "I've been thinking of taking an apprentice for some time."

Jendaline almost managed to keep her mouth from dropping open. "A--apprentice?"

Renas looked at her. "Why not? You seem eager to study aeromancy, and I have the little house out back. It's designed for an apprentice. And as for character....well, Taran travels with you, and that's character reference enough for me." He shrugged. "It's yours if you want it."

"You--I mean, thank you! Thank you very much!"

Renas inclined his head. "And thank you."

An awkward silence fell. Renas turned to his brother, his face suddenly grave. "Taran, I know why you have come."

Taran's surprise couldn't be hidden. "You....do?"

"I do." Renas regarded him evenly. Taran couldn't hold the gaze, and studied the floor. Jendaline looked back and forth between them, but seemed to sense that she did not belong in this conversation. "The attack woke me as well, the night that it happened. I could tell something was wrong, but I didn't know what." He folded his hands on his lap, suddenly seeming very interested in his fingernails. "So I sent my mind out on the winds. I saw firsthand the fate of Feldwar, and of our parents."

Grief welled up in Taran's chest. "I--I'm sorry. I don't know what to say."

"Three days ago, I wouldn't have known either. But I've had three days to grieve, three days to consider all that I witnessed that night. And I think that now I do know what to say. What happened in Feldwar was not your fault. I don't know much about it, but I do know that."

"Thank you." Taran's voice cracked.

"I don't want to intrude," Jendaline said hesitantly, "but what did happen in Feldwar?"

"Yes," Renas interjected, "I've been hoping you could answer that question for me as well."

Taran sighed. "I don't really know what happened. I dreamed I was approached by a necromancer named Aseligan, and he tried to kill me with a pestilence wave. The pestilence was real. Feldwar was destroyed."

Jendaline stared at him in wide-eyed silence. Renas leaned forward, frowning. "I don't understand, Taran. Why would Aseligan try to destroy you?"

Taran looked at the floor, then at Renas. He wished he and his brother were alone, but could think of no real reason why Jendaline couldn't hear what he had to say. "That's part of the reason I came here. Renas, did you ever have any--strange experiences during your training?"

Renas laughed. "Sure I did. Every time Pop tried to teach me aquamancy, I had strange experiences involving the great Renas and failure."

Taran swallowed. His voice sounded hoarse and weak. "No, Renas--I mean *really* strange." He shifted uncomfortably in his chair.

Renas set his tea on the table. "No, Taran, I don't believe I have. Why do you ask?"

Taran sighed in frustration. Renas had been his last hope of finding someone who could help him--someone like himself. "Because I have. Because that's why I think Aseligan attacked me--because I can *do* things."

Renas frowned. "Do things? I'm not sure I follow you."

Taran looked at his feet. "I only know one word for it, Renas, and you won't believe it." His brother's look challenged him. "Okay. Sorcery. I don't know what else to call myself but a sorcerer. I can make things disappear, I can create things out of nothing, I can instantly move things from one place to another." He took a long, shaky breath.

"My brother the sorcerer, eh? That's really wild. Could you-- could you do something, then? Demonstrate, somehow?"

"I wish I could, but I've had the strangest problem since leaving the Feldwar. I haven't been able to cast the simplest spell. I couldn't even light my campfire without using my staff." He laughed harshly. "Wouldn't that be ironic; to nearly be killed because of extraordinary powers only to immediately lose them?"

"Now, now, let's not jump to conclusions." Renas leaned back in his chair. "I doubt it's anything that drastic. You say you had to use your staff on the fire....have you ever had to use your staff for your spells before?"

"No....actually my staff was never out of my closet, really," Taran admitted with some chagrin.

"Okay--so the staff is out of the equation. Then how--I know," he said with a sudden laugh. "Taran, did you bring a crystal?"

Taran's eyes widened. "Oh, Darkness, no. No wonder I can't cast any spells...." His eyes drifted to Jendaline, searching for the familiar crystal around her neck He frowned. "Jendaline, how do you heal without a focusing crystal?"

Jendaline was trying not to laugh at him, and it was obvious. She reached into her pocket and produced a little leather bag, in which Taran found the caramel-colored crystal on a silken string. "Of course I have one, Taran, I just keep it packed up when I travel."

Taran sighed. "But I don't have one. I'm just an apprentice, remember?"

"Oh, that's right." Renas winced and shook his head. "Dumbest thing I ever heard of, not giving crystals to apprentices. How do you expect them to do anything at all?"

"That's the idea," Taran replied. "Keep the apprentices out of trouble; the only time they can cast spells is when the master wizard allows his own crystal to attune to the student." He laughed. "Seems effective to me."

Renas shook his head again. "I still say its completely backwards." He walked over to his desk, searching through the drawers. "Withhold from a student a simple tool that would allow him to practice and hone his skills, but give him a staff. Darkness and damnation, wizards can strike a man dead with nothing but a staff! And yet it's perfectly safe to turn apprentices loose with a staff, but Light save us if we give them focusing crystals so maybe they can actually do what we're training them to do." He pulled a clear crystal on a black string from a desk drawer and handed it to Taran. "Here you go, little brother. It's an aeromancer's crystal, of course, so I don't know how it will work for a sorcerer posing as an aquamancer, but maybe it will be better than nothing."

Taran held the glittering crystal up in the light, wondering what color it would turn when he attuned it to himself. The color of a crystal reflected its owner's specialty; blue for aquamancy, green for geomancy, clear for aeromancy, red for pyromancy, black for necromancy, and caramel brown for healing. He couldn't imagine what color would represent sorcery. "Thank you, Renas. How do I--how do I attune it?"

Renas shook his head again. "The things they don't teach you," he snorted. "Attuning a crystal--a little detail, eh?" He considered a moment. "Usually attuning a crystal involves bringing the element of your specialty to bear on it. I don't know what that would involve for a sorcerer, but I can tell you how an aeromancer does it."

"Might as well give it a try," Taran said. "What do I have to do?"

"First off, hang on a second while I release my crystal. You're going to have to use it for your spell." Renas closed his eyes a moment and concentrated. "Okay, now hold the crystal out in front of you. Bring up the air currents below it to support it so you can let it go."

Jendaline watched silently from her chair as Taran frowned, holding the crystal in front of him and trying to recall basic aeromancy. "Remember," Renas said, "it's just like aquamancy, only you're dealing with currents in air instead of water." Taran smiled; his mother had used the same words. He slowly pulled his hand away from the crystal. It trembled, then floated steadily.

Renas nodded. "Good. Now pull the air around it in a slow cyclone--think of it as a whirlpool of air. But do it slowly. And don't drop the crystal."

Taran closed his eyes, trying to pull the air in long, slow circles around the crystal without dropping the support underneath. He couldn't see what happened, but he heard Renas behind him. "Very good. I can see Mom got hold of you sometime. Now step back a little--you don't want to get caught in this."

Taran did, and his brother continued. "Now pick up the speed. Pull the air around it faster. Okay, faster still. Good. Now faster."

For what felt to Taran like forever, the sound of rushing wind filled his ears. The passage of time could only be marked by his brother's voice saying "faster" at regular intervals. Finally, Renas said, "Okay, that's good, Taran, you can stop now." Taran dropped the spells and crumpled to the floor, mopping at the sweat on his face. The crystal, suddenly devoid of enchantments, fell. Renas had seen all this before. He caught the crystal in midair.

"Darkness!" Renas breathed, turning to where his brother lay, his head in Jendaline's lap. "Taran, what did you *do?*"

"I--just what you told me to," Taran gasped, struggling to sit up. "Why?"

"Well, I did say I didn't know how it would work for a sorcerer," Renas said wryly, holding up the crystal.

The crystal glittered smoky gray.

*****

A few hours later, the three shared a dinner of roast pheasant with vegetables and fresh bread. Taran relished the taste of his first real meal in three days.

"My brother the sorcerer," Renas said, shaking his head. "When word of this gets out...."

"I know," Taran groaned. "That's what I'm afraid of. I'm afraid I am going to need to build a place away from the village."

Renas nodded slowly. "I think you are right. I would be glad to put you up here, of course, but your abilities won't be secret for very long if you stay here in town. The local commons always keep a close eye on 'those wizard's houses' anyway--we're suspect, you know, can never be entirely trusted--and it won't be long before everyone knows all about the village sorcerer."

Taran chewed a moment, considering this. "I don't have much choice, then. I don't even know what I can do. I certainly don't need local commons speculating on my abilities."

"First thing tomorrow, then," Renas said, "you need to scout yourself out some land and we'll take you to the town council building to register your claim."

"What about the registration fee?" Taran asked in alarm. "I'm running low on coin at the moment."

Renas laughed. "For you, there will be no fee. Things are a little different in Caleb--wizards aren't trusted here. We are quite respected, mind you, but along with that respect is a healthy dose of fear. The Council, which is entirely commons, would never dream of charging an aquamancer for land on which to live. After all, you might summon a typhoon, or a drought, or something equally horrible."

"But I would never--" Taran protested with his mouth full.

"Of course you wouldn't," Renas agreed, "but how are they supposed to know that? The difference between Light and Dark wizards is extremely hard for a common to see." He shrugged. "So a few details like land fees are taken care of for you. But I'm afraid you are going to have to do better than those robes. An apprentice aquamancer isn't likely to command respect from anyone."

Taran bridled at this remark. "It ought to command respect from anyone who isn't a master aquamancer." Jendaline choked on a mouthful of vegetables, and Renas shook his head. Taran sighed in resignation. "I can change the color of these easily enough. What shall I be?"

Renas considered that. "Yes, going as a sorcerer would hardly help you. Why not go as an aquamancer? That is what you are trained as, after all."

Taran nodded, and when Renas looked over at him his white apprentice robes were suddenly deep sparkling blue. Renas whistled in admiration. "Nicely done, little brother. I would say that certainly qualifies as sorcery."

Which means I certainly qualify as a sorcerer. The thought for some reason destroyed the comfortable feeling of belonging, and left him feeling cut adrift and alone once more.

*****

Taran worked late with Renas and Jendaline, making the apprentice house suitable for occupation by an actual apprentice. Taran could see the little house had been used before, but he could also see it had happened long before Renas came here.

Taran and Renas scrubbed the walls, and Jendaline cleaned the floor. "It seems to me that with two wizards in the room, this cleaning ought to be much easier," she remarked.

Taran smiled as he knelt beside a bucket of warm soapy water to rinse out his rag. That sort of thought had occurred to him often during his training. Healers weren't taught much wizardry theory, though.

"That's actually a very common misconception," Renas said, in what Taran thought of as his 'instructor' tone. "I think it has its root in the fact that most people don't understand what a wizard's power is. Once you know where a wizard's power comes from, you see right away that there are certain things we just cannot do.

"A wizard draws his power from nature. Each discipline of

wizardry is bound to a particular facet of nature, and the magic that wizard practices consists of manipulating that particular facet. For example, I'm an aeromancer--a wizard of air. I could summon a windstorm to blow the dirt out of here--and very likely blow the house down around us as well. But I couldn't just magick the dirt into thin air; it's beyond the boundaries of wizardry. So cleaning the house with a wizard is the same as cleaning house with a housemaid." Renas paused. "Now cleaning house with a *sorcerer* on the other hand...." His meaningful glance made Taran laugh.

Jendaline sat back on her heels and dropped her rag in the nearest bucket of water. "The difference between a sorcerer and a wizard wasn't clear to me at first, but I think I'm beginning to understand. Are you saying Taran is not bound by those rules? He *can* just make things disappear?"

Taran nodded slowly, feeling awed by the idea himself. "It seems unreal, doesn't it?"

Jendaline pushed her damp hair out of her eyes. "Then why in Darkness are we doing this? Why don't you just magick it all done for us?"

Taran wished she hadn't asked that. Explanations of theory came hard to him. He looked pleadingly at his older brother.

"It isn't quite that easy, Jendaline. We've settled that Taran *can* do things outside the normal boundaries of wizardry. What Taran has to settle with himself is when and whether he *should.*"

Jendaline looked utterly lost. Taran realized that he and his brother both shared the perspective of their father's teaching, and she did not. "I guess what we have been getting at," he said slowly, "is that sorcery is not natural. So it upsets nature when I do it." He paused, sorting out his thoughts. "You can imagine nature as a tapestry, woven of different colored threads for the different facets; blue, white, red, green, black, and brown. When wizards practice, they nudge those threads. They change the tapestry slightly, but the tapestry is still unmistakably there. Healers, like yourself, nudge the brown ones. Renas uses the white. When I do aquamancy, I use blue. Do you see?"

Jendaline nodded slowly. "What happens when you cast a sorcery?"

Taran sighed. "When I cast a sorcery, I force my hands through the tapestry and shove all the threads aside."

Had Jendaline really gone pale, or was it just a trick of the light? "So you're creating *holes* in--in *nature?*"

"It isn't as bad as it sounds." Renas seemed amused. "They are not permanent holes, and I don't think the process is quite that violent. But the fact remains that sorcery is fundamentally different from wizardry, and we don't know yet what the repercussions may be."

"Plus," Taran interjected, "it's really tiring."

Jendaline and Renas looked at each other and laughed. Taran looked from one to the other and wondered what was so funny.

*****

Shortly after dawn the next morning, the three went scouting for land. They ended up farther from town than Taran had hoped, but as Renas optimistically observed, that made it less likely that anything they saw had already been claimed.

An electric tingle shot through Taran, and his head snapped up. Sheer rock cliffs surrounded them on three sides, neatly outlining a piece of property the perfect size for a cottage and a garden. The small clearing in the middle extended to the back wall, where there was a cave in the rock. Tall, thick trees covered the rest of the property. A clear, cold stream ran out of the cave and down the property.

"This is it," Taran said suddenly. "This is the place."

Renas and Jendaline looked at him in surprise. "Here, little brother?" Renas asked, with a gesture encompassing the clearing. "Are you planning on living in the cave?"

Jendaline tried to hide her laughter behind her hand, and Taran felt his face turn red. "Here," he insisted, embarrassment notwithstanding. "It has to be here."

"It's okay, Tar," Renas said with a smile. "I was teasing you. This is a beautiful piece of land." He reached into his saddlebag for the red wooden stakes. "Set these at the corners and we'll go register your claim in town."

*****

The Council Building was squat and stocky, made of an odd assortment of mismatched rocks. Inside was a hallway from which several rooms opened. Taran searched out the sign reading "Claim Registration". He started that way, but Renas pulled him in the opposite direction.

"Wizard Registration?" Taran read from the sign. "What in Darkness is that?"

"The Town Council tracks how many wizards are in Caleb." Renas held open the door.

"But that's the most ridiculous thing I ever heard of!"

Renas followed his younger brother into the office, forcing a smile. *"Please* keep your voice down," he hissed through gritted teeth. "I told you this isn't Feldwar. Let that be enough for now, please, and let's get you registered."

Taran didn't understand why Renas was so upset. He followed without comment to the registration counter. "Mage Renas," the clerk greeted the aeromancer with a respectful tilt of the head.

"Good morrow," Renas replied. "I have two new registrants for you today."

The clerk nodded politely, and pulled two papers from a small drawer beside him. He turned to Jendaline with a warm smile. "What be your name, magice?"

"Jendaline. I'm a healer from Hommel."

"Wonderful. We can always use healers." The clerk scribbled on the paper a moment, apparently recording this information, then turned to Taran. "And you?"

"Taran. Aquamancer. Feldwar." Taran wondered if the clerk would have been warmer with him had he been a female as attractive as Jendaline. The clerk nodded, looked for something else in his drawer, and scribbled some more. Finally he handed each of them a thick parchment card. "Mages, thank you for your time and support." The clerk turned from them.

Taran glanced at the card in his hand, and showed it to Jendaline as they exited the small office. "How about that? We're card-carrying members of Caleb's Registered Wizards Club."

Renas shrugged eloquently, leading them to the claims office. "It's one of the marvelous benefits of registration." He held the door for them.

Taran was almost to the polished wooden counter before he realized he was alone. Renas and Jendaline were absorbed in quiet conversation, pointing at a map on the wall, so he moved to the counter by himself. Unsure what else to do, he placed his new card on the counter. "I would like to register a claim, please."

The girl behind the counter examined his card for a moment, and smiled. "Well, mage, you've come to the right place." She reached under the counter for a thin parchment map. "I just need you to indicate on here what you have found and where, and the land-master will be out tomorrow to register it."

"Thank you." He pulled the map closer and accepted a carefully sharpened charcoal marking stick. The maps were hand-drawn by the local mapmaker's apprentices. He studied it a moment, and finally located the clearing in front of the cave. In thick black charcoal lines he marked a square he hoped was roughly the same size as the property he'd seen. The quality of the map being what it was, scale was difficult for him to determine. The cave at the back of the property was clearly indicated on the map, and he suddenly noticed something odd about the way it was marked. A strange red mark had been placed deep within the cave's interior, and though he examined the map for several more moments, he couldn't seem to find any indication of what that red mark might mean. Finally he returned the map and the marking stick to the girl behind the counter, and moved across the room to the large wall map that Renas and Jendaline were still examining.

The cave, and the strange red mark, were both marked on this map as well. He frowned as he addressed his brother. "Renas, what is this mark?" He pointed to the red slash in the cave.

Renas studied the mark a moment, and turned abruptly away. "I'm sure it's nothing, Taran."

Taran frowned after him, confused by his behavior and strangely bothered by that mysterious red mark.

"Try not to worry about it," Jendaline offered, patting his shoulder. "There's no need to let it bother you. It may not mean anything at all."

He couldn't argue with her, but neither could he see why anyone would take the trouble to mark every copy of the local maps with an identical red mark if it didn't mean anything at all. He doubted they would have used red if it was anything good, either. Red was a universal color of warning, and he couldn't help but wonder, had he seen a map before he saw the property, if he would have gone there at all.

*****

Taran was still thinking about the strange map when they went to a local inn for the noon meal. "The Ram's Head Inn and Tavern," he read from the sign. There was a simple picture of a ram's head below the text. "Charming."

Renas laughed lightly. "Well, the name may not be much, but the food is very good." He held the door open for Jendaline and his younger brother.

"Good," Taran replied, sitting down at a table towards the back. "I don't know about you two, but I am starved."

"Yes, I know," Renas said with evident amusement. "One would think you never get to eat." He caught the attention of a serving girl and waved her over.

She took in their robes casually and stood beside their table, an empty tray propped negligently on one hip. "What'll it be for ye?"

Her accent was strong, her consonants thick, her dialect much less refined than the people they had talked to in the Council Building. A common, obviously, and a poorly educated one at that. But then, what else did you find serving tables in a tavern in a relatively poor town?

"Berry juice for the magice," Renas told her, "cider for....him, and herb tea for myself."

She nodded curtly. "And to eat?"

Renas considered briefly. "A tray of cheeses, please, and some berries, and a few loaves of that wonderful dark bread."

She nodded again. With a slight inclination of her head that may or may not have been courteous, the girl walked back toward what Taran could only assume was the kitchen. Her walk was stiff, and she stared straight ahead as she moved.

"Is it my imagination," Taran ventured hesitantly, "or did she seem--"

"Not so loudly please, brother," Renas said conversationally, a placid smile frozen on his face. "Yes, she did seem a little less than pleased to see us. She wasn't rude, though, so it hardly bears commenting on. I've told you this isn't Feldwar. Wizards are not trusted by all, and there are those who would not have us permitted in town at all." He shrugged. "A certain amount of that feeling is simply distrust for things they don't understand, of course, but you must also remember that wizards have done more harm than good for Caleb in the past. Only after seeing the examples of Feldwar and Grillom has the council here decided to welcome wizards at all, however provisionally."

The serving girl approached with their drinks, and he paused while she thumped them on the table, never looking any of them in the eye. "Thank you," Renas told her, and seemed to mean it.

The girl glanced at him briefly, surprised, and dropped a nod in his direction before she turned to leave. "Ye're very welcome, mage." Her tone was a little warmer than before. "I'll have yer food out soon."

Renas carefully sipped his tea until she was out of earshot. "There are, of course, many wizards who will not tolerate the attitude they find here. Many have stayed here only briefly, moving on to one of the more forward-thinking towns where wizards are welcomed and respected. Who knows, coming from the backgrounds you two have, you may soon tire of the feeling here as well, and want to go back. I can't blame you. But on the other hand, I can't blame the townsfolk here for feeling as they do, and if a few wizards don't stay here, Caleb will always be easy, defenseless prey for the wizards of the Dark."

"In time their feelings may change," Jendaline offered, her voice low and casual. "They don't have much experience living in the sort of town they are trying to build." She reached for her juice, then lowered it to the table without tasting it. "I think they are very brave to even try. What reason have they to trust us, after all? And it's easy to see how they could resent us. Even the worst of wizards has a better education than almost any common. When you travel to an all-wizard town, like Jarek, you rarely see pictures such as these on the signs. They aren't necessary; everyone who lives there can read. Why, any of us have probably seen more education in the first month of our apprenticeships than that girl has seen in her entire life!"

"Or is likely to see for the rest of her life, either," Renas agreed. "I'm sure she does resent us being here, and having to serve us, even if only a little. Hopefully as time passes and more and more wizards settle here and contribute to the town, at least some of that resentment will fade. Whether they realize it or not--whether they like it or not--Caleb needs wizards in the worst way, if for nothing more than to offer some defense against other wizards."

Taran sipped at his cider, realizing he had lived a very sheltered life. Renas had an excellent understanding of a state of affairs Taran hadn't imagined could exist. Jendaline, whom he naively imagined had never been beyond the gates of Hommel before, evidently had traveled as far as Jarek--wherever that was-- an all-wizard town. Yet another concept he hadn't known existed. He considered the possibilities of this as his eyes took in the rest of the room. A town populated entirely of wizards! A town where pictures on signs were unnecessary, because all who lived there could read. He frowned. What of the visitors? Wizards wouldn't matter, of course, any wizard who visited would obviously know how to read--but what of the commons?

The serving girl arrived, with their food spread on her

ever-present tray. The group watched without comment as she laid the trays on the table and departed.

"Such a serious frown for such a nice meal," Renas observed, reaching for a slice of the dark bread. "What's on your mind?"

"What of the commons?" Taran asked, and it took the blank looks on the faces of the other two to remind him that Jarek was not the main topic of conversation. He blushed and tried again. "I mean, what of the visitors to Jarek who are not wizards? Without pictures on the signs, how do they find anything?"

His brother's fond smile told him he had once again overlooked something in his thinking. "Given the feeling toward wizards here and in countless other towns, how many commons do you think are likely to go out of their way to visit a town completely comprised of wizards?"

"Oh," Taran said, for lack of anything better to say.

Jendaline also smiled. "But you are right, it isn't as if they never have commoner visitors in Jarek. It is a rather prominent seaport, as well-protected as you can imagine it is. The Town Council there has prepared special maps, marked with the pictures that would otherwise be on the signs. You can pick them up in the Council Building there."

"I think it's just a kind of snobbery that drove them not to put the pictures up in the first place," Renas said, and Taran could see his point. "They must have wanted to emphasize to visitors--and to themselves--that they are in a town full of highly educated people. Not being able to read and moving though streets with nothing but words on the signs would certainly remind you constantly that you were in the presence of great power, and keep you feeling inferior until the moment you left.

They must have known that when they made their decision for pictureless signs in Jarek."

"I don't know," Taran said mildly, slathering butter on a thick slice of bread. "Maybe they didn't consider anything like that at all. After all, everyone who lived there was a wizard, and everyone who was going to live there would be a wizard. Maybe they felt it was insulting to a group of people with that level of education to live in a place with pictures which are intended as a crutch for less educated people. Maybe they were just trying to make it as appealing a place for wizards to live as possible, to attract as many as they could. They did make the maps, after all, and they hardly would have done that if they were trying to make commons feel unwelcome, or to keep them out altogether."

"You do have a point." Renas didn't sound convinced.

The serving girl returned once again, to ask them if they needed anything else. The trays and their mugs were almost empty, but Renas shook his head. "We were just finishing up."

"Thank ye, mage." She moved toward a table near the door, where the girl from the Council Building and a man Taran did not know sat down.

"Well, kids, are we done here?" Renas asked, moving as if to rise.

Taran had eaten almost too much. He nodded and looked at Jendaline. She pushed back her chair. "Where are we going now?"

Renas dropped a silver on the table to cover the cost of their meal. "After this we are going to the merchant's shop just down the road from here. There are several things we are going to need to buy to get you settled into the apprentice's quarters. We are also going to need to stop by the seamstress and order a few apprentice gowns for you." She looked surprised, and he quickly continued. "I know, you're a healer, and you have outgrown apprentice robes. That's what you think. As long as you are my apprentice, the town is going to need to be able to identify you as such. Unfortunately, it's back into apprentice gowns for you, Jendaline."

Taran left an extra two coppers by his mug. He tried not to be noticeable in the gesture, but he could tell Renas had noticed nonetheless. His brother made no comment though, until they are out on the street. "Why the coppers, brother?"

Taran flushed. "I was thinking about what you said; how wizards have brought more harm than good to Caleb, and how the serving girl probably resented us being there. It isn't fair that we should have so much more education by luck of birth, and it isn't her fault that we are wizards and she is frightened of wizards. She did a good job for us, and I want her to know I appreciate it, even if a lot of wizards she's seen have not."

"But I thought you were low on coins."

"I am." Taran's tone was defensive. "But not too low to make a gesture of goodwill. If people here can learn to expect something more than destruction from wizards, their misgivings will fade much faster."

"Relax, Taran," Renas said with a smile. "I'm not criticizing you. I think it was a fine gesture."

Taran wondered why making such a fine gesture should make him feel like a thing on display, but he said nothing.

*****

After lunch they went to a general shop. Dry goods, tools, and housewares lined the walls, and large bins brimmed with every manner of thing a person might need. The short, balding merchant nodded to them from behind the counter. "Good morrow, mage Renas. What need ye today?"

Renas nodded in return. "A few necessities to get my new apprentice settled in her quarters. I expect my brother the aquamancer will also be needing some things. He starts work on a house soon."

"Ah." The merchant's eyes lit up at the prospect of a sale. "Building a house, are ye? Well, old Mavel has all the things ye'll be needing, young mage. Come in whenever ye like. Wizards maybe ain't exactly what Caleb needs, but coin is coin. A merchant can't live on philosophies alone."

"Thank you." Taran turned to inspect the nearest row of shelves. He knew 'old Mavel' hoped to sell him all of the lumber and materials he needed to build his house, but as low on coin as he was, buying lumber was simply out of the question. His land was well-stocked with trees, and he planned to fell some of those. Even so, he did need many things, such as the tools with which to shape the trees into lumber suitable for building. He looked carefully at two handsaws, wondering how many of the things he needed he could afford.

"As ye're selecting yer goods, young mage," Mavel offered, "ye'll want to keep in mind that wizards pay half of what is written."

Taran's eyebrows raised in surprise. "Thank you again," he said sincerely.

"Yet another reason why Mavel's is my favorite shop," Renas said with good humor. "I'm sorry I forgot to mention that to you, brother."

Mavel shrugged happily. "A little detail, eh?"

With the discount Mavel offered him, Taran decided to purchase the more expensive of the two handsaws, since its better quality more than justified the higher price. He placed the handsaw on Mavel's counter, and turned to a bin of small forged iron nails.

When he finished, Taran had set aside quite a pile of merchandise. "This should get me started," he told Mavel.

Mavel's eyes gleamed. "Aye, it certainly should. Four golds should cover it."

Again the merchant had surprised Taran. The goods were easily worth eight and a half golds, and as much as he appreciated the mistake in his favor, he could not in good conscience cheat the man. "Are you sure? Even at half the marked prices--"

"There should be more than four golds here," Mavel finished for him. "Don't fret it, young mage, ye're not cheating old Mavel. Though I'm right pleased ye had the goodness to ask. Four golds is yer price, young mage." He turned to Renas with a broad wink. "Mage Renas, I like this brother of yers more with each minute. A good lad he is. A right good lad!"

"He certainly is," Renas said from beside his own stack of goods.

Taran wondered why being such a good lad should make him feel a thing on display. He drew four golds from his coin pouch, and handed them to Mavel. "Shall I have these things sent to yer place, young mage?"

"Yes--that would make things much easier for me. It's a lot about an hour's ride north of town, a clearing next to the rock face of the mountain--"

"Ah," Mavel interjected with understanding. "By the cave."

"Yes." Something in the merchant's tone made Tarn frown. "By the cave."

Mavel nodded. "It's brave ye are, young mage, building by the Crystal Cave. Heed old Mavel's advice, now, and stay out of there. Crystal Cave ain't but trouble. In fact, I've heard it said that--"

"Mavel!" Renas cut in sharply. He didn't sound like himself at all, and Taran looked at him curiously. "I need your assistance over here, I believe my apprentice has finished shopping." Jendaline had picked out some light blue cloth for curtains, several towels, a set of pots, a small water bin, marking sticks and paper, soap, and some simple dishes. Without comment Taran handed her an oilcloth from a shelf beside him, and she smiled as she added it to the pile. Without her healer's leathers, she would certainly need it.

Mavel did some calculating in his head. "Four golds and a halfsilver, mage Renas." Whatever generosity had prompted his discounted price to Taran evidently did not extend to his older brother. Still, the price was very good. Renas directed the merchant to deliver his purchases to his home, and the group left the merchant's shop.

"You must let me repay you," Jendaline told Renas, fumbling for her coin purse.

"Hah, you'll not tell me what I must or must not be doing, apprentice." He leaned on the word. "If we are going to do this, we're going to do it right. Your living quarters, food, and basic necessities I will provide. Anything on top of that is your own affair, based on what coin you can bring in for yourself. Fair enough?"

"It's the way it's been done for generations," she said wryly. "I could hardly argue. But Renas, I'm not an ordinary apprentice. I am, after all, a healer, and have been for some time. I can certainly pay my own living expenses."

"Not while you are my apprentice, you don't." His tone brooked no opposition. "Look at it this way, there's no sense in aggravating the townsfolk's suspicions, right?"

Jendaline sighed in resignation. "No, I suppose not."

"You may as well accept it," Taran told her quietly. "He isn't going to give in. I've seen Renas's stubborn side before."

Jendaline gave him a weak smile and said nothing more as they entered the seamstress's shop. The seamstress, a woman only slightly taller than Mavel but substantially wider, was finishing up a gown on a polished wood dress form. She laid down her needle and went to meet them, rubbing her hands on her apron. "Mage Renas. How nice to see you again. What brings you in today?"

Renas inclined his head. "Sephya, I would like you to meet my new apprentice, Jendaline, and my brother, the aquamancer Taran."

Sephya nodded to each of them in turn, and turned back to Renas. "You'll be needing apprentice robes for the magice, then?"

"Absolutely," Renas told her. "About half a dozen, I think. I shouldn't wonder if Taran would like to order some robes as well. He has just traveled from his home village, and I imagine his are pretty well worn."

"Yes, yes, I definitely will be needing some new robes." Taran only had one aquamancer's robe, and it would be better to have new ones made in the usual fashion than to magick himself more. Taran had decided that sorcery was something to use as little as possible, especially until he could figure out what the ill effects were, both on himself and everything else.

"Very well," Sephya said, "if you will follow me, magice, we'll get your measurements and I will start on these just as soon as I can."

Jendaline followed the stout seamstress into a small room, leaving Renas and Taran standing in the main room, where various types and colors of cloth were displayed.

"Sephya and Mavel are good folk," Renas remarked quietly. "Given a choice, I would always take their establishments over any of their competitors here in the village. They are honest traders and will serve you well, wizard or no."

"Why do you think Mavel sold those goods to me for so much less than their worth?" Taran said, just as quietly. "That seems out of character for any merchant."

Renas shrugged. "You are starting work on a home. Mavel knows if he does you a good turn now, he will see plenty more of you later. Besides that, I think the man just likes you. He certainly wouldn't have done that for just any newcomer who walked into his shop needing supplies."

Taran nodded; the logic of enticing him back for future purchases made sense. Regardless, it was a stroke of good luck for Taran, and he was duly grateful.

A short time later the measurements were complete, and Renas and his brother settled their bills. Renas gave Sephya six silvers to cover the six robes he ordered for Jendaline. Taran decided that three robes would suffice for him. He reached for his coin purse to pay, but Sephya waved a hand at him.

"There's no charge for wizard's robes, young mage," she said. Taran was surprised once again. When Renas had told him "a few little details like land fees are taken care of for you," Taran never dreamed he meant this much. A few little details apparently meant land fees, robes, and half of whatever general goods he needed. He appreciated it, and yet he couldn't help feeling guilty. Why should living cost him less than commons, who all worked as hard as him, and some harder, for their coin? Small wonder wizards weren't welcomed here!

*****

Scarcely a month later, Taran and Jendaline were wed. Her apprenticeship in aeromancy had been going well. Renas stood as witness in their small ceremony, watching them through oddly slitted eyes. It reminded Taran of his brother's odd behavior in town. Jendaline moved into the little cabin in front of the cave, continued her studies, and Taran didn't think any more about Renas until he saw those oddly slitted eyes again.

It was the same expression Taran saw a couple months later when he first told his brother Jendaline was pregnant.

*****

The sun angling through the bedroom window into his eyes woke Taran early. Before he even got out of bed, the silence of the house seemed to ring in his ears, giving him the clear impression that something was wrong. He sat on the edge of the bed, rubbing at his eyes. There was no reason to think that way-- sure, it was Sunday, Jendaline's day off, but she was probably outside, or sitting in the kitchen. Quiet did not necessarily mean trouble.

A vivid memory assaulted his mind, a memory of waking up in his room in Feldwar in the middle of the night to a silent house and an acridly sweet smell on his tongue.

He ran through the little house, his alarm rising. Jendaline was nowhere to be seen. Bread and cheese were laid out in the kitchen, evidence of her preparation of breakfast. Juice and cider sat in sweating pitchers on the table, and herb tea in a pot.

There were three mugs on the table.

Taran frowned. Why on earth would Jendaline have put out three mugs? Unless someone else had been there--someone familiar, someone who would not be out of place at the breakfast table.

Sweat slicked his palms. He couldn't think of a logical reason why he should be so upset, but there it was. He ran outside.

His wife was not in the yard. Both horses stood placidly munching oats in the little stable--so Jendaline couldn't have gone to town. A third horse was tethered to a nearby tree, pulling leaves off one of the bushes. Each saddlebag bore a white cloud emblem.

Renas's horse?

It fit well with his earlier observations. So Renas had come by early that morning, while Jendaline was preparing breakfast in the kitchen. Then what?

This time of year, Jen liked fresh fruit with breakfast, so he started toward the yellow apple tree. Her red wicker basket was there, lying on its side on the ground. Four apples had rolled out of it.

Taran's heart pounded in his ears. What now, what now? He couldn't think straight. Something was very wrong. And yet-- what on earth could have overtaken a master aeromancer and his apprentice?

Aseligan.

He saw with perfect clarity the distorted shapes in the bed in the house in Feldwar, could feel the air so thick with the stench of death that it choked him. His vision went black.

No--he didn't have time for fainting. He fought it off. Somewhere out there, that son of a dog had his wife and his brother. Aseligan had robbed him of his entire life once before. Taran wasn't about to let it happen again.

But what could he do, how could he help them? Even using sorcery, he couldn't magick back two people when he had no idea where they were. He had to locate them first. Then he would worry about getting them back.

He focused suddenly on the stream. He didn't have time to experiment with ways of finding them--years of practice had made him adept at doing that with aquamancy. He closed his eyes, and sent his mind downstream.

Nothing. The water carried no impressions. Two or three

times he looked out from the stream but saw nothing along the banks to indicate anybody had been there at all.

With dread, he went back the other way--upstream, into the Crystal Cave. Almost immediately he picked up an impression. Renas and Jendaline had crossed the stream here. The impression glowed orange--still fairly fresh. Maybe an hour old.

He concentrated, delving deeper into the impression. Jendaline struggled, both hands pinned behind her back in her attacker's ruthless grasp. She dragged them through the stream deliberately, with the thought of leaving tracks for Taran. Her attacker tried equally hard to keep away from the water, also thinking of the impressions they would leave.

But Renas? Where was Renas?

He pushed harder into the impression. Jendaline's impression dominated, but he fought past it to examine the impression of the forceful presence lurking behind her, propelling her into the cave. His thoughts were oddly shielded, but Taran could discern distinct physical features. This was a tall man, narrow of build, with dark eyes creased by deep laugh lines.

Renas had abducted Jendaline.

The realization crashed into Taran with the force of a physical blow, and he sank beneath it. Betrayal more bitter than this could not be possible.

He somehow managed to scrape together the strength to send his mind deeper down the stream, farther into the cave. He found a few more impressions, fainter than the first. Renas had evidently grown better at keeping Jendaline away from the water. Surely they weren't much farther now...just a little more....

His mind hit a wall of lightning. It shot deep into his brain, knocking him onto his face in the muddy soil at the edge of the stream. Taran pushed himself slowly out of the mud, wiping the grime from his eyes as he sat painfully up. Never had he encountered a ward so strong! He had not known Renas was capable of such powerful magic.

Abruptly his despair twisted, hardened into rage, and his anger drove him to his feet, and into the Crystal Cave. The ward precluded any use of sorcery to magick Jendaline out of there. Brother or not, Taran would hunt Renas down.

And when Taran found him, no ward on earth would save him.

*****

Taran crept through Crystal Cave as quickly as he dared, moving as quietly as he could. His mental crash into the ward had probably already alerted Renas; he tried desperately not to give any other signals of his approach. Judging from what he could remember of his trip up the stream, he had probably covered a little over half of the distance.

The slight sound of a footfall ahead of him froze Taran in place. He strained his ears, standing perfectly still, listening for the tiniest sound. He heard nothing but his heart pounding in his ears.

He finally dared to release the breath he was holding. Immediately a soft voice floated to him. "Taran?"

Ice stabbed through his middle. That voice...it couldn't be...

And yet he couldn't be mistaken. That voice sang in his earliest memories, recited stories through his childhood, told him the valuable lessons of aeromancy that stayed with him still. He held his torch aloft, peering out ahead of him.

Karran stepped hesitantly out into the light. "Taran? Taran, what are you doing here?"

Taran stared at her, heedless of the tears running down his face. "Mother..." How was this possible? "Mother, I--"

"No." She cut him off, shaking her head. "The Crystal Caves are dangerous, Taran. You shouldn't be here. You belong in Feldwar, with your father and me."

"Father?" Taran's voice cracked, and he sobbed.

"Oh, Taran." Sympathy warmed Karran's voice, and she pulled him close, hugging him to her. He could smell the scent of lavender that always clung to her. "This hasn't been easy for you, I know. Come with me. I'll take you home, and all will be well."

Taran wanted to acquiesce. He couldn't remember the last time he had felt so safe; his mother's presence enfolded him like a blanket. And yet he could not. "No. I can't give up. My wife, and my child--I have to save them."

His mother's hands on his back curved, clawed like talons through the fabric of his shirt. "You little mongrel!" The voice was no longer Karran's. It grated, like ground glass crunching. "If you will not leave, you will die!"

Taran struggled, and managed to shove the thing away from him. It tore gashes across his back, and he stumbled backwards. "Light!"

His mother's corpse faced him, brandishing the skinless bones of its fingers like weapons. He stared with horror at the unholy thing, grateful that the flickering torch did not produce much light. This--this was an atrocity far beyond the capabilities of his brother. This had to be Aseligan's handiwork.

Taran backed up against the slick. mossy cave wall, putting a few steps of distance between himself and the corpse. What could he do? This thing would not tire, would not cease until it killed him. He knew nothing of necromancy.

He closed his eyes, holding the torch in front of him like a shield, and tentatively reached out to the thing with his mind. There was nothing there; this corpse had been reanimated and had a single-minded purpose--to destroy him. He reached deeper, surrounded that command with his mind, and gritting his teeth, squashed it.

The corpse blew apart, splattering him with gore and slamming his head into the rock. His vision swam, and he slid down the wall to the floor.

Unconsciousness danced before him; a tempting abyss of welcoming darkness. He had had all he wanted of this crazy adventure; why Aseligan should hunt him was a mystery, and Taran had no idea how he could defeat the dark wizard, even if he managed to find him. He could crawl into that darkness and find relief--perhaps if he dove to the bottom of it he would never resurface.

But he couldn't let himself do it. Somewhere in this cave was his wife, and with her the tiny life she carried, calling out to him for help. Scattered on the cold ground around him were the bones of his mother, who by any just reckoning should be tending her lavender gardens in Feldwar. And the person responsible for these things hid behind a magical ward, farther down this very path. Taran would find him.

And neither Light nor Darkness would save him then.

*****

The grueling journey through the Crystal Cave could have taken days, or even years. Taran lost all sense of time in that horrible place; one minute blurred into the next, and the next, until he could hardly remember a time when he had been anywhere else. The gore splattered on his clothes and in his hair stank, and his stomach churned whenever the slight breeze shifted and blew the reek back into his face. He had splashed through the stream a few times, hoping to wash some of it away.

Eventually the narrow, jagged corridor widened, and he was

startled to find the passage blocked by a gray, formless mass. He reached tentatively out with his senses to touch it, and it bounced him right back into his own mind with a shock.

He shook his head briskly, regarding the gray blur. This had to be the ward he had encountered earlier. A visible ward was a new thing in his experience. He reached out his hand; to his surprise it passed easily through. A ward not to prevent physical passage, then, but magic. This did not bode well. What other tricks did Aseligan have planned that Taran had never heard of?

It didn't matter. There was nothing for it but to plow ahead and hope for the best. Jendaline and their baby were depending on him. With a deep breath for courage, Taran pushed through the gray ward.

"Ah, sorcerer-boy has decided to grace us with his presence." The booming, resonating voice sent a chill of memory through Taran's brain. He had only heard it once before, but he would never forget. "Welcome to the Cavern of the Crystal Altar, sorcerer-boy!"

Taran's eyes tore through the cavern, trying to take in everything at once. The cavern was roughly round, with a towering high ceiling and walls that sloped away out of sight. Torches flickered from stands, and the large pond in the middle of the cavern glimmered in their light. The stream disappeared into the pond. Huge, glittering crystal formations covered the walls and dipped down from the ceiling--crystals that bounced light and magic equally effortlessly, and did not need to be attuned. The formations were both beautiful and terrifying, but the most awesome formation was in the middle of the pond. A giant, wide crystal formation jutted from the surface of the water, like a sparkling table. This was the Crystal Altar, for which the cavern was named.

Jendaline lay motionless on the Crystal Altar, bound by ropes that glowed with magic. He brushed her with his senses--she lived, but could not move or make use of her magic.

To the left side of the pond, Aseligan regarded him with a theatrical sigh. The necromancer looked just as Taran remembered him, tall and imposing in his dark robes. "You are quite persistent, my young friend. Annoyingly persistent. The lad can't take a hint, can he, my dear Renas?"

Taran followed the wizard's gesture across the pond. His brother stood at the water's edge, motionless, staring without seeing. "Renas!" Taran took a step toward him and halted. How deeply involved was Renas in this? What kind of role did he play?

Renas did not respond. Not even a flicker of recognition crossed his face; his gaze passed unchanged through his brother.

"You are wasting your breath, sorcerer-boy. Renas has better allies than you these days." An obscene grin cracked the necromancer's face. "A man takes a certain risk sending his mind into a pestilence wave, you know."

"You! You have done this thing to my brother. You've stolen my wife, killed my parents. Why?"

Aseligan chuckled, setting Taran's teeth on edge. "Do you really think this is all about you? I suppose it must appear so, to one who knows no better. In truth, sorcerer-boy, it is you who are confounding my plans. Have you heard of the Ritual of Eternity?"

Taran shook his head.

"I would have expected as much," Aseligan said, waving his hand as though Taran's ignorance was a matter of no import to him. "I have been preparing for the Ritual for two years. And when I consulted with the spirits of the dead, I discovered that there lived but one man who could oppose me. And I managed to learn his name. And now, despite my efforts to the contrary, I find that man standing here, interfering at the exact moment when I must perform the Ritual!"

"I don't care about your damned Ritual. All I want is my wife."

Aseligan laughed out loud. "Your ignorance is amazing, sorcerer-boy. The Ritual of Eternity grants immortality by transferring a life-force to the necromancer who performs it. An *unused* life-force. And where else would you find an unused life-force, but in an unborn child?"

Taran couldn't breathe. It seemed to him he heard Jendaline moan. "You *bastard,*" he hissed. "You would sacrifice my wife, and my child, so that you can live forever?"

"Look at that, he *can* be taught! My dear sorcerer friend, this woman's pregnancy is the only reason I did not attack you after you left Feldwar. The spirits of the dead can be wonderful sources of information, if only one asks the proper questions." He glanced at the altar. "This has been a charming reunion, sorcerer-boy, but I am on a strict schedule. So I say to you again--goodbye, Taran--forever!"

Aseligan threw his arms into the air. Taran braced himself, ready to cast a ward, but no pestilence wave rolled forth this time. Instead, a lumbering mass of half-rotten bodies trudged into view behind Aseligan, plodding slowly but steadily toward Taran. He sucked in his breath--he *knew* these people! The entire population of Feldwar staggered toward him--somewhere in that gruesome mob of corpses was his own father.

Darkness, he should have foreseen something like this. What could he do? He glanced at his brother. "Renas--Renas, I know you are in there, somewhere. I really need your help!"

Renas did not move. He stood like a statue, looking out over the pond, across Jendaline at Aseligan. Taran thought his brother probably awaited the dark wizard's command.

He stepped farther away from Renas, scrambling for a coherent thought. Perspiration stung the gouges in his back, painful reminders of the last time he had encountered one of these reanimated foes. He couldn't possibly fight them all one by one as he had his mother; they would shred him to pieces long before he finished. In desperation, he closed his eyes and turned to sorcery, throwing his rage out in the form of a wall of flame.

Aseligan managed to throw up a ward. The army of corpses, however, burned and smoked in columns of reeking fire. Relief surged through Taran--until he realized their steady advance had not stopped. Unholy shrieks echoed from the crystal formations as the burning corpses staggered forward.

Light! What on earth should he do now? In a panic, he reached out and crushed the directive driving the nearest of the corpses. It exploded, and the force of it shattered several of the corpses near it. Encouraged by this, Taran picked another target and crushed it as well.

This wasn't going to cut it--already he was short of breath, and maybe ten of the army had fallen. The population of Feldwar had been around a hundred--he didn't know if he could last long enough to defeat them all, even assuming they didn't kill him first. He picked another corpse, and as it blew apart he saw a few others fall in various places, finally succumbing to the flames.

They could burn to death! It was the first lucky break he'd had--when the fire had initially failed to stop them, he had thought all hope was lost. Maybe with that working in his favor, he could manage to survive this after all. He couldn't forget that Aseligan continued in his preparations for the Ritual. Even if Taran managed to defeat the army of undead, all would still be lost if Aseligan completed the ritual first.

With renewed vigor, Taran targeted and destroyed individual corpses. A handful at a time, they dropped.

Aseligan raised his arms and began to chant. Blackness dropped like an impenetrable curtain in front of Taran's eyes, and he cried out. Aseligan must have cast Blindness. Taran had lost his sight, until Aseligan released his spell or died. A pit of sudden despair opened in his stomach. How could he battle a wizard he couldn't even see?

A final few corpses had managed to lumber on long enough to attack him. The searing heat blistered his arms and face. Naked bones raked through his skin like talons, and dead arms crashed into him like clubs. Taran struggled with every fiber of his being to maintain his concentration, to cast the final sorcery that would destroy these last four corpses.

The explosion threw Taran backward to the rocky ground. He hit his head, and a wave of vertigo washed over him. He clutched at the rocks, desperate to regain his equilibrium.

"This has gone on quite long enough," Aseligan snarled. "I had hoped not to expend much energy on you, sorcerer-boy, but you have become quite a nuisance. This will destroy you once and for all!" He began to chant, and when Taran heard the first few words of the spell, he knew this was the end. "Ashes to ashes...." Aseligan was casting Dust.

"Renas!" Taran cried. He had no hope of dodging a spell in this condition. His limbs trembled and he couldn't muster up the strength to stand. Casting a ward was out of the question. His lost brother was his last hope. "Renas, please! Help me!"

Taran huddled in the rocks on the floor of the cavern, unable to see, trying to interpret the muddled impressions of his ears. He could hear the sizzle of the Dust spell, and the roar of a giant wind. Screams echoed in the cavern, and water splashed.

All was silence.

Slowly Taran's vision cleared, and he managed to stand, squinting in the light. Jendaline sat up on the Crystal Altar, slowly, as if every motion was painful. He stared at her, afraid to believe the danger had passed. "What happened?"

"Renas." Her voice sounded husky from disuse. "He summoned a wind behind Aseligan. It blew him into the pond."

"But--the Dust? That would have blown the Dust right over you!"

"I know." Her gaze flicked to the shore. "Renas cast a ward over me."

Taran's eyes widened with sudden understanding. "Oh--Renas..." He followed her gaze, but no sign of his brother remained.

"He didn't have time to cast two wards," she said brokenly. "He didn't have the strength to cast one large enough for both of us, especially when he was fighting to keep Aseligan out of his mind at the same time."

"Renas." Taran couldn't seem to speak coherently. His brother had sacrificed himself to save Jendaline and the baby.

A splash from the pond jerked Taran's attention back to the present. A shaking, clawing hand reached for the shore.

Aseligan was climbing out of the water.

"Not today," Taran muttered, throwing his arms in the air. He wasn't sure how this was possible--Aseligan should have been dead, since his Blindness and Restrain spells had released. Perhaps he had simply lacked the strength to maintain them and save himself. Taran wasn't concerned about the particulars of the situation. He cast Vortex.

A spinning, sucking whirlpool opened in the surface of the

pond, pulling the necromancer under. Taran chanted Seal under his breath, and collapsed back onto the rocky ground, exhausted. With grim satisfaction, he watched the surface of the water thicken and glassify. Nothing could break that surface now, as long as Taran lived.

The hands clawed frantically at the surface, then fell away.

*****

Taran's unnatural wounds healed slowly, but under Jendaline's care they did heal. A statue of Renas had been erected in the village square in Caleb. The town, which had been so divided in opinion about wizards, seemed to interpret the affair of the Crystal Cave as a warning. If there had been no wizards living in Caleb, Aseligan might have succeeded. And so the statue of Renas was not simply a memorial, but also a sign of the changing attitudes of the townsfolk. Taran thought his brother would have been pleased to see it.

A rebuilding effort had begun in Feldwar. People from several villages in the area had relocated there to help with the cleanup and rebuilding. Taran's house in Feldwar was the first building scheduled for official reopening; he and Jendaline had already been invited to the ceremony. The house would be used as a school for multi-specialty wizards.

Taran and Jendaline became the Guardians of the Crystal Cave, in part because of their roles in stopping Aseligan, and in part because of the convenient location of their house. The Crystal Cavern, because of its amazing crystal formations that amplified magic and required no attuning, was the only known location where powerful spells like the Ritual of Eternity could be cast. For the moment Taran had cast an aeromancy Seal across the entrance to the cave. Because aeromancy was not his strong point, he had also cast a ward over the entrance, to alert them if anyone attempted to enter the cave. The spells would last until the end of Taran's days. And perhaps then he would be reunited with his family again.

He could face them now, without shame. The Sorcerer had avenged them all.

The Crystal Cavern

Sandra Miller

The Crystal Cavern

Excerpt from the novella *The Enemy in the Mirror* by Sandra Miller

Until I rounded the corner of the engineering building and saw the rocket chair hovering in the university courtyard, I guess I thought I was used to the idea of Allacore attacks. I thought, like so many around me, that I knew everything there was to know about them. But an Allacore too lazy to fly? I despised them, but this was a new low even for them. This Allacore must have stood over ten feet tall--if she ever got out of that flying chair of hers long enough to stand. Her wings must have been curled against her back, because I couldn't see any evidence of them at all. The splintered ragged tips of her unkempt talons jutted out even when they were retracted. Her close-cropped white hair looked like it hadn't been washed in weeks. Their snowy white wing feathers and their equally white hair were the most attractive features Allacores had, if the word attractive could even be used, but on her neither were visible. Her gold metal armor must have been a sight to behold when it was new. At this point, though, it was dingy and pitted, and only added to her overall impression of disrepair.

Allacore. Just the name was enough to make my skin crawl, and here was one in my hometown! I stood there in shock as she hovered over the university path, herding students just like me into the holding cells that had been set up on the grass. We were out of her direct line of sight for the moment, but all too soon I knew we would be following our glassy-eyed peers into those dismal little cells. The Allacore mind-control devices were efficient. We were only spared the effect because we had not been there when she fired it. But she could handle the two of us easily enough. After that, who knew? Hard labor in their factories, servitude in their homes, forced indenture on their small attack ships--any of a hundred unpleasant fates could await this newest group of prisoners once they were taken back to the enormous generation ship that had brought the Allacore here, the generation ship that even now orbited Earth.

I glanced at Trevyn standing there beside me, his face a picture of shock as he surveyed the scene playing in front of us, fresh out of a nightmare. Of course we had all heard about the Allacore raids, but who expected them this far inland, here in the middle of nowhere?

Before I had recovered my wits, Trevyn had let go of my hand and was striding purposefully toward the Allacore's hovering chair. I should have guessed he would do something of the sort--Trevyn never could stand by and watch injustice. The battle may have been doomed, but he was determined to fight it, even unarmed. He would not go quietly, like the groups of hypnotized students around him.

"Commander! I demand that you cease this at once!" Trevyn's voice rang off the nearby buildings. I found time to wonder how he had known the Allacore's rank--I should have guessed that politically minded Trevyn would have been studying the Allacore raids much more intensively than I.

The rockets under the Allacore's chair glowed red as she swiveled it around to face Trevyn--and me behind him. I shivered under that emotionless stare; she regarded us as if we were so many bugs. "You demand?" Her voice grated like ground glass crunching under boots. "You? Who are you to demand anything of me?"

"I am Trevyn Blaine, and I am a citizen of this free country, a country which does not allow the sort of acts you are committing here." I stood as if my feet were rooted to the spot, horrified. *Oh, please God, don't let her kill him,* I implored in my mind.

The Allacore's face clouded with rage. "Filthy human!" she spat. "I'll teach you some manners, you rude little bastard." Her ragged talons were fully extended now, and she reached for the directional control on her chair.

The tension building in me was suddenly too much to bear. The capture of hundreds of students shocked me, but did not spur me to action; my own death I could have accepted with hardly a protest. But when she turned against Trevyn I could stand there no longer. Acting completely out of an instinct I hadn't known I possessed, I balled my right hand into a fist and held it high over my head. "Enough!" I cried, and against her will the Allacore found her attention pulled from Trevyn and focused entirely on me.

"Enough?" Her tone was syrupy sweet. Her broken, yellowed teeth flashed at me as she smiled a condescending smile. "Enough of what, human? I haven't yet begun!"

If she had dropped her superiority attitude and really looked at me, she would have noticed the bright yellow light streaming from beneath my curled fingers, pouring from between my knuckles. But she didn't see, and I held my hand clenched in that fist for a moment longer. "I command you to stop!" I shrieked, and to my surprise my voice echoed and re-echoed, even stronger than Trevyn's had a moment before. Before the Allacore commander recovered from her surprise, I pulled back my arm and flung it out towards her, opening my hand. The ball of light that left my grasp was like a miniature sun, racing toward her too fast for the eye to follow. It crashed into her chair and sent it reeling, casting scorch marks deep into her battered armor.

If I could have kept my wits about me, I would have grabbed

Trevyn and run right then. But I was stunned, absolutely unable to believe what I had just done. I stood there gaping in disbelief while she brought her runaway chair under control and veered back toward me, whipping out a strange device that resembled a telescope. "So we have a powerful little monster here," she grated. "So this trip will be considerably more worthwhile than I had imagined. Your power will benefit me greatly, human." She leveled the telescope-thing at me, and it began to hum.

It was plain from her words that the thing was stealing whatever strange power I had, but I felt as though it was leeching all my energy. My knees buckled and I fell onto the sidewalk, marshaling everything I had for one last strike. This time when I flung out my shaking hand, no miniature sun burst forth. The Allacore laughed an ungodly laugh when she saw the wispy stream of light that issued from my palm--but she stopped laughing when the tendril of light wrapped itself around her telescope-thing and snatched it from her grasp. I jerked my hand to my chest, and the light recoiled, pulling the telescope-thing into my palm with a satisfying slap. "No, Allacore," I told her, leveling the device at her, "I think it is your power that will benefit me." The device hummed louder than before, and she began to shriek.

I was bursting with energy. I could have run a marathon, and I suppose at that point I should have stopped. I was past caring about the welfare of this despicable Allacore, though, and I noticed that her shrieks had gotten the attention of the masses of students around me. As she weakened, they came forth from the cells, broke out of the mindless lines they had been herded into, and encouraged by this, I held the device steady. The hum was deafening now, drowning out the Allacore's unholy screams. The device was shaking so hard that I needed both hands to hold it.

All at once the Allacore was silent. Her body seemed to

crumble, to collapse in on itself--and then she was gone. The chair crashed to the ground and lay still, sitting at a sharp, broken angle. On the grassy field where hundreds of people had been prisoners only moments before there was silence, and then the cheering started. Grateful students surged out of the holding cells and toward me, cheering their happiness, their thanks. I knelt panting there on the path, the telescope-thing hanging useless from my hand, stunned. It was Trevyn who reached me first, Trevyn who pulled me to my feet and started dragging me away from the crowd. "We have got to get you out of here, Ellane!" he shouted over the noise, and the alarm in his tone brought me back to my senses. Without questioning why, I ran with him, following him away from the university campus and the masses of students who had so narrowly avoided capture.

*****

Visit Sandra Miller on the web at
www.sandra-miller.com

Email:
sandra@sandra-miller.com

www.ingramcontent.com/pod-product-compliance
Lightning Source LLC
Chambersburg PA
CBHW020649130626
46552CB00003B/1466